ART & MAX

To Dinah!

This edition published in Great Britain in 2011 by Andersen Press Ltd., 20 Vauxhall Bridge Road, London SW1V 2SA.

First published in USA in 2010 by Clarion Books.

Published in Australia by Random House Australia Pty., Level 3, 100 Pacific Highway, North Sydney, NSW 2060.

Text and Illustration copyright © David Wiesner, 2010.

Printed and bound in Singapore by Tien Wah Press.

David Wiesner has used acrylic, pastel, watercolour and India ink in this book.

10   9   8   7   6   5   4   3   2   1

British Library Cataloguing in Publication Data available.

ISBN 978 1 84939 266 2 (Hardback) ISBN 978 1 84939 267 9 (Paperback)

This book has been printed on acid-free paper

ART & MAX

DAVID WIESNER

ANDERSEN PRESS

The name is Arthur.

I can paint too, Arthur!

You, Max? Don't be ridiculous.

Well...you could paint me.

You? Really?

What are you doing?

I'm painting you!

Ta-da! What do you think?

This is preposterous!

Ooh! Turn around—
I missed a spot.

Wow!

Oh, Max...

...what have you done?

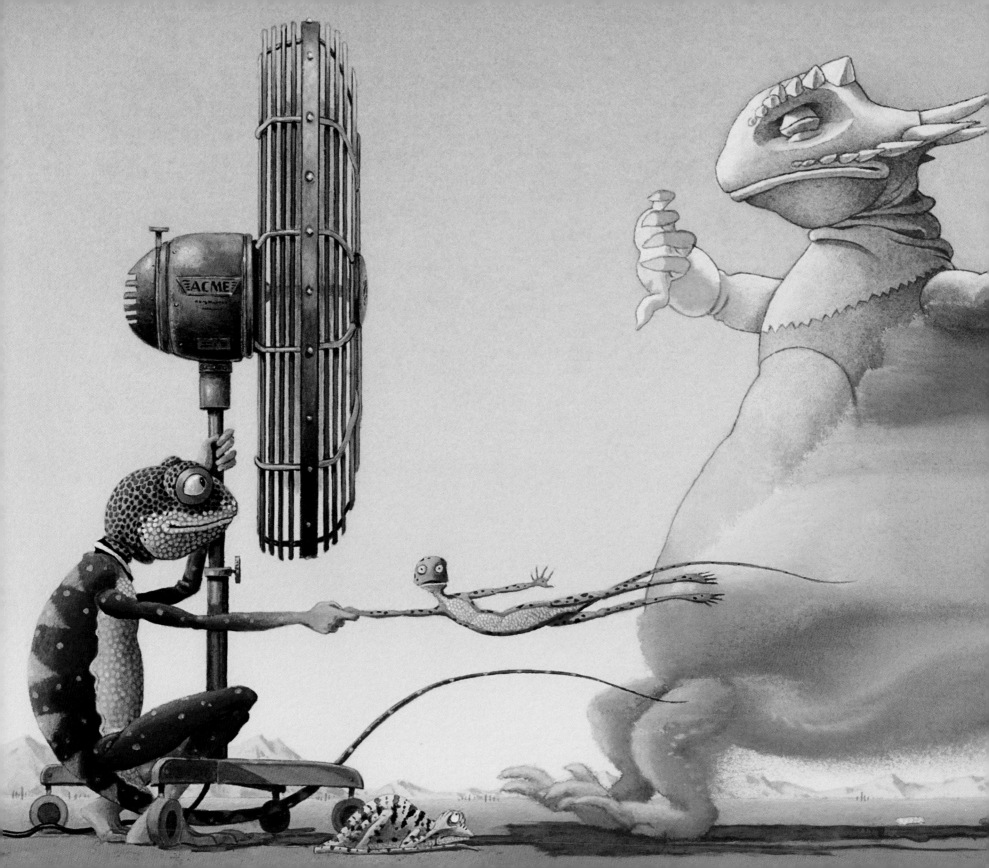

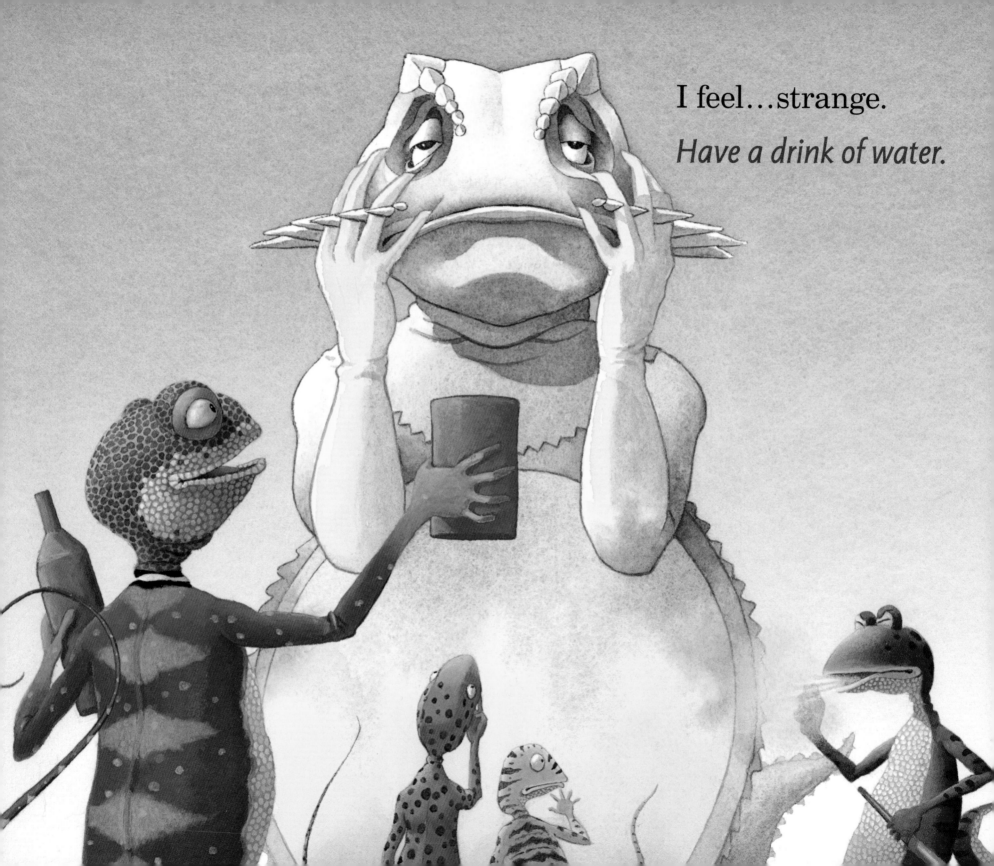

I'll get some more!

Hold on, Art—

It's *Arthur!*

Don't go…

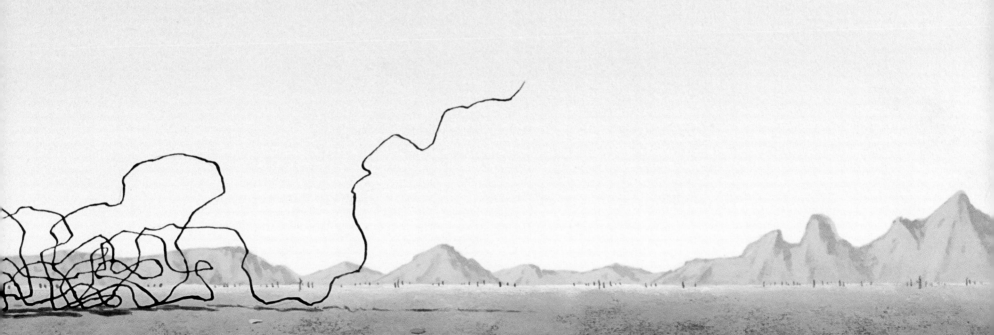

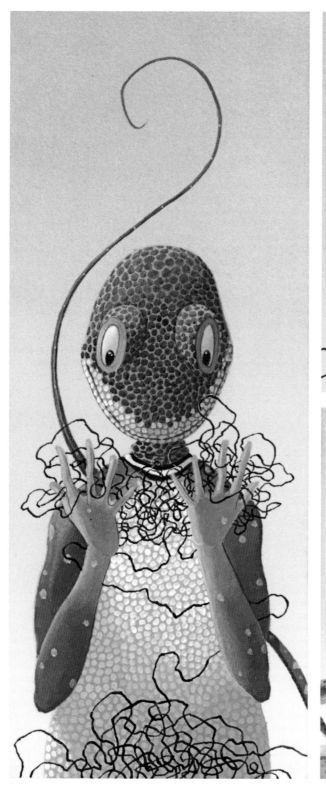

Aha!

OK, here goes!

More detail, I think.

How's that?

Acceptable, I suppose.
But don't forget my foot.

Come back here!
You're not finished!

Now what?

Just hold still, Arthur!

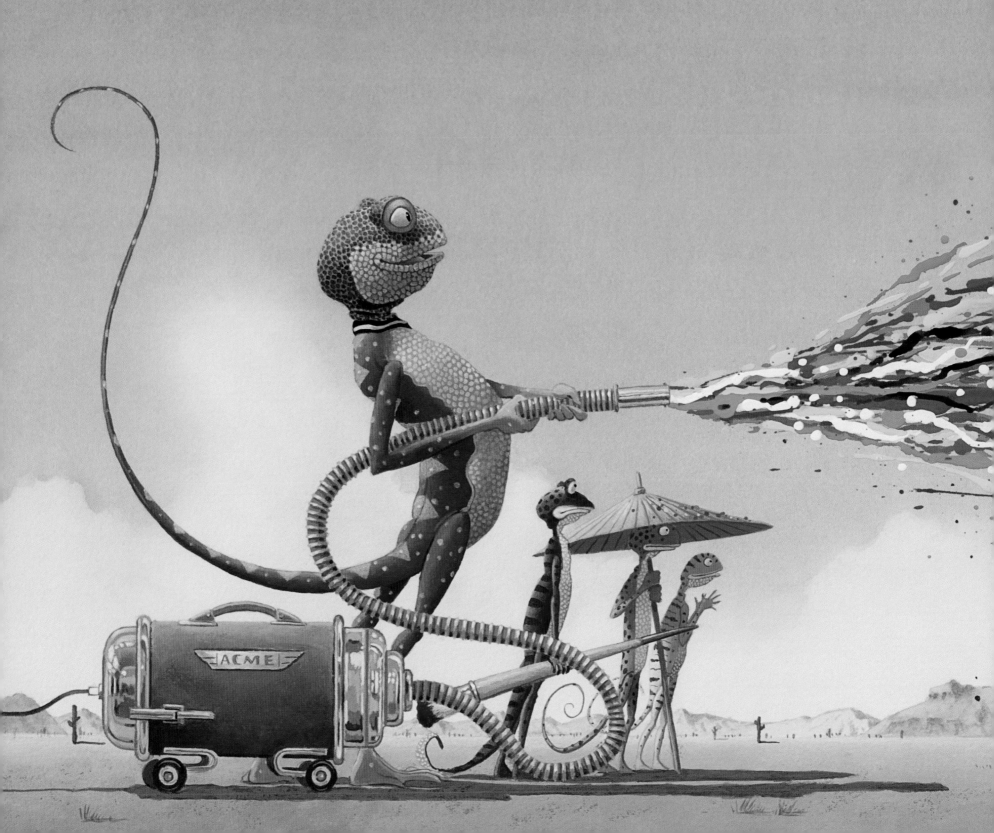

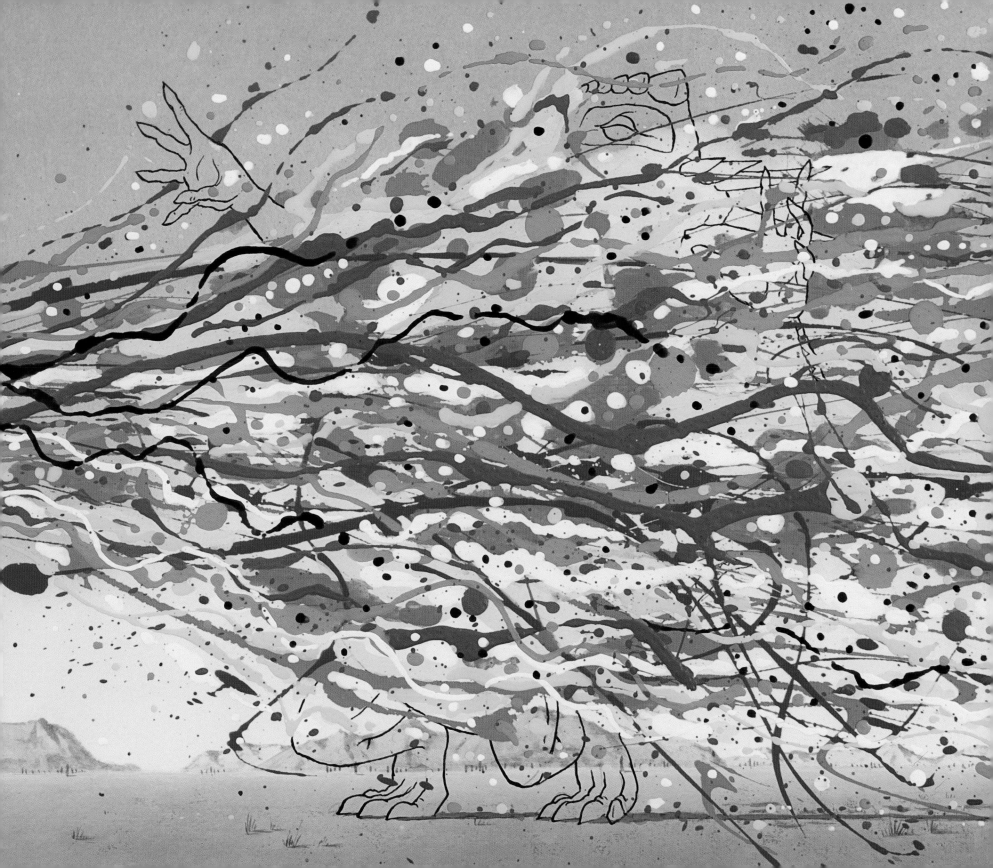

Fascinating.

Yes! Yay!

Let's paint some more!

All right, Max,
let's get started.